The Wish Fairy

Fairies Forever

ALSO BY LISA ANN SCOTT

The Wish Fairy

ENCHANTED PONY ACADEMY

The Wish Fairy

Fairies Forever

Lisa Ann Scott

illustrated by
Heather Burns

SCHOLASTIC INC.

Text copyright © 2018 by Lisa Ann Scott
Illustrations by Heather Burns, © 2018 Scholastic Inc.

ISBN 978-1-338-12105-6

10 9 8 7 6 5 4 3 2   18 19 20 21 22

Printed in the U.S.A.   40

First printing 2018

Book design by Yaffa Jaskoll

To my BFF, Vic.
Thanks for all your support.
Couldn't wish for a better bestie!

Chapter 1

"I just came up with the most amazing wish ever," Brooke said as she sat with her best friend, Izzy, and Calla the fairy. "I definitely saved the best for last."

"What is it? Tell me!" Izzy begged.

Calla raised an eyebrow. "The best wish ever? Oh, I do hope you're right this time." The tiny fairy hovered in the air.

They were gathered in the meadow behind Brooke's house, right where it all had started. Brooke had rescued Calla from her cat, Patches, and got seven wishes in return. It was the law of Calla's land, Fairvana. Seven wishes for a life spared— but they all had to be granted in two short weeks. Time had almost run out.

Brooke's first wish for one hundred cats had to be reversed with a second wish to return them to their owners. She didn't realize the kitties had disappeared from good homes until missing cat posters popped up all over town! Her third wish for buried treasure left everyone greedily digging in her meadow, so she donated the gold to the library.

Her fourth wish was to sing the solo perfectly in the school concert, but that didn't make her a great singer. Just great at one song. Her fifth wish to be popular meant she had no time for Izzy. So to become unpopular, Brooke raised her hand in front of the whole class and asked the teacher for extra homework. But to make sure that didn't *really* happen, she spent her sixth wish asking for *no* homework. Then everyone started failing their tests!

After all that, Brooke wasn't even sure she wanted to make her final wish—until she came up with the best one ever.

"True, my wishes haven't worked out quite like I'd planned," Brooke said, flicking a flower head into the grass for her cat to chase. Patches scampered after it. "But I know this one will be amazing. It has to be. It's my last one."

Izzy bounced on her toes, clutching her hands in front of her. "Please, please, make the wish!"

Brooke cleared her throat. "Calla, I want to visit Fairvana with you and Izzy. Right now."

"Seriously? Woo-hoo!" Izzy squealed and twirled until she tumbled onto the flowery field.

Calla's eyes were wide. "I wasn't expecting that."

"But you can do it, right?" Brooke asked.

Calla landed on the big flat rock in the field. She paced back and forth, thinking.

Patches and Izzy's cat, Pumpkin, charged through the field and jumped onto the rock next to her.

Calla squeaked in surprise, but the cats just curled up next to her. The fairy patted Pumpkin's tail affectionately. She was no longer deathly afraid of the cats like she had been at first.

"I suppose I can grant that wish," Calla said. "I imagine all the fairies will be so excited to see real humans, maybe they'll

finally want to be friends with me!" She flew up into the air and spun around. "Go ahead, then, make your wish!"

Brooke got goose bumps as she silently rehearsed the words a few times. She was a bit sad this was the last time she'd be making a wish that would come true. Even if they didn't always turn out quite right, making wishes had been exciting.

Brooke practiced it in her head, then said, "I wish Izzy and I could visit you in Fairvana right now, with everything we need, and have a super exciting time, and that no one would miss us at home." She turned to Izzy. "I'm not leaving anything out, am I?"

"I think you covered it," Izzy said. "This is going to be great!"

"I know! So that's my final wish, Calla!" Brooke said.

"I'm happy to grant it!" Calla said.

There was a big, glittery flash of light. And suddenly, Brooke and Izzy were floating in the air!

"We're flying!" Brooke said. They hovered above the rock where the cats slept. She kicked her legs, then looked over her shoulder. "And we have wings!"

"Of course! How else could you fly to Fairvana?" Calla asked.

"And we're tiny like you!" Izzy said, examining her arm.

"You'd destroy Fairvana if you showed up as giant humans." Calla laughed. "Come on, it'll take a while to fly there."

"Wait, are you sure no one is going to miss us while we're gone?" Brooke asked.

"Time on this side of the forest is paused until we return," Calla said. "See?"

Brooke looked around her. On the rock, Patches was perfectly still. A butterfly hung in the air, unmoving. The leaves rustling in the breeze were frozen in place.

"Wow," Brooke whispered.

"Your wish totally came true!" Izzy said.

"I hope this wish works out!" Brooke said.

"It already has," Izzy cried. "This is perfect!"

Brooke and Izzy high-fived.

"Wait!" Calla said. "I've been wanting to do that forever!" She held up her hand so Brooke and Izzy could high-five her, too. "Woo-hoo!" Calla said.

"Let's go!" Brooke yelled. "This is going to be so much fun!"

Calla laughed. "You'll probably never want to come back home!"

Chapter 2

Brooke and Izzy flew through the air, following Calla into the woods behind Brooke's house.

The forest was cool and dark compared to the big, sunny field. And the trees seemed enormous now. Taller than skyscrapers. The girls buzzed by a bird who was bigger than them!

Calla zoomed ahead, in between the trees.

"Wait for us!" Izzy hollered. "It's our first time flying."

Calla slowed down and waited for them to catch up.

Brooke quickly realized her delicate wings flapped in response to her thoughts. If she wanted to go faster, they moved faster. If she wanted to stop, they stopped. "I can't believe we can fly."

"It would take far too long to walk to Fairvana," Calla said. "Do watch out for goblins along the way."

"Goblins?" Izzy whispered.

Calla nodded. "The deeper we get into the woods, the more magical creatures you'll see. Not all of them are nice."

They flew along, Calla going more slowly

as they went farther. She pointed out wood sprites hiding in the trees, then a unicorn grazing on forest lilies.

"Be quiet so we don't spook it away," Calla whispered as they spied on it from a tree limb far above. "They're incredibly rare."

They watched the majestic creature for a while and then flew on. Even though Brooke was excited to reach Fairvana, she couldn't shake the feeling that something about her wish had been wrong. *What did I miss?* she wondered.

The noises in the forest changed as they got deeper inside it. Strange grumbles and groans filled the air as they approached a stream.

"Oh no." Calla frowned. "Trolls. They're going to demand payment for us to cross the bridge over the stream."

"But we're flying. We don't need to use the bridge," Brooke pointed out.

"It doesn't matter. If we pass this way, they want payment. They'll throw rocks at us. Usually, I can zip by unseen. But I'm not sure you two will be fast enough. I guess we'll just try to sneak by from tree to tree." Calla flew to a tree and hid among the leaves.

Brooke and Izzy followed, but they were much slower.

"What's that?" one of the trolls bellowed, pointing straight up at them.

"Is someone trying to sneak by without

paying a toll?" asked another. He hurled a rock into the tree where the girls were hiding.

Brooke and Izzy caught up to Calla and huddled behind the leaves with her. "What should we do?" Brooke asked.

"Stay put for now. If we fly to the next tree, they could hit us mid-flight. They have pretty good aim," Calla said.

A rock whizzed through the air above them. Another bounced off the trunk below. Brooke and Izzy clutched hands. "I'm scared," Izzy whispered.

"This wasn't what I meant when I wished for an exciting trip!" Brooke said.

Then *whomp!* A big stone hit their branch, sending the three of them tumbling toward the ground!

Calla quickly caught the wind on her wings, and then grabbed Brooke and Izzy by the hands, just before they crashed.

"Thanks!" Brooke cried. Maybe she should have added *"Safely* visit Fairvana" to her wish!

Izzy looked too stunned to say anything.

They stood on the ground in front of the trolls. "We don't have anything to pay your toll," Calla said. "Let us pass."

The trolls laughed. "That's not how it works. No payment, no passing. You'll have to work for us to earn your way."

Brooke and Izzy shared a terrified look. "What kind of work?" Brooke asked.

The troll shrugged. "Busting up rocks. Cutting down trees. Nothing too hard."

"I'll go get three sledgehammers," the other troll said.

As Brooke, Izzy, and Calla huddled together, three tiny men in green suits hopped out of the woods.

"Look! It's the leprechauns who were after your gold!" Izzy whispered.

"You trolls wouldn't be holding on to some of our gold, now, would you?" asked the leprechaun who Brooke remembered was named Fitzgibbons.

The two trolls held their hands up in the air. "No, we don't have gold. Not any of yours!"

The leprechaun named McMurtagh

leaned toward Calla, Brooke, and Izzy. "Go, while they're distracted!" he whispered.

"Thanks!" Brooke whispered. Her new wings flapped a few times. It was still hard to believe she had wings and could fly. They were so light, she almost forgot they were there. She rose into the air with Izzy and Calla and they darted out of sight.

"That was scary," Izzy said, once they got deeper into the forest.

"Leprechauns have hearts as good as their gold, if they consider you a friend," Calla told them.

They flew on for a while without any more excitement, which was fine with Brooke. Then Calla stopped flying and hovered midair.

"What's wrong now?" Brooke imagined goblins or gremlins waiting for them next. An enchanted forest sounded like a wonderful thing—until you ran into the bad guys.

"Nothing's wrong." Calla flew around a big tree and hovered in the air. "We're here. Fairvana is just ahead."

"That's great!" Izzy said. "Why do you look so nervous?"

"I'm not sure they'll be happy to see the three of us."

"Why?" Brooke asked.

"No human has ever visited Fairvana before. I'm not even sure it's allowed."

Chapter 3

"Why didn't you tell me that when I made my wish?" Brooke asked. She didn't want to be mad at the fairy, but Brooke was frustrated. After all, she could've added something to the wish so she and Izzy would be welcome in Calla's home!

Calla bowed her head. "I was just so excited—and so sure that if I brought you to Fairvana, the fairies would see how wonderful humans can be." She lowered her voice. "And I thought if they saw you two liked me, the fairies might want to be friends with me, too."

Brooke and Izzy shared a worried look. "What will they do to us if they don't want us here?" Brooke asked.

Calla shrugged. "We'll find out soon enough. Come on. This is the only way in and out of Fairvana. An invisible shield around our kingdom keeps out other creatures."

Brooke was nervous, so she reached for Izzy's hand. They flew between two enormous trees that stood together, the branches arched to make a small opening. There was barely room to squeeze through.

Even though she still felt worried, the sight on the other side made Brooke's jaw drop. She didn't know what to say.

"Fairvana," Izzy whispered in awe.

Tiny houses were nestled in among the mossy roots of big trees. Some were perched on low branches. Smoke puffed out of chimneys, and yellow windows glowed in the dusk.

Little carts made from tiny old birds' nests were parked outside the houses, full of flower petals, pussy willows, different

seeds, and berries. Rings of mushrooms surrounded campfires. Rope bridges connected the trees.

"This is adorable!" Izzy squealed.

A pebbled path wound through the forest floor among the trees. Acorn lanterns hung along the path, illuminating it. The ground was covered with moss, ferns, and

flowers. A small stream bubbled past the little village in the distance. Blue lights winked in the trees.

Brooke pointed to them. "Wisps!" The mischievous glowing creatures had helped them scare away the treasure hunters who'd invaded her meadow looking for gold.

"It's even more amazing than I ever imagined!" Izzy said.

"I know!" Brooke agreed. There were so many lovely details to take in. Brooke had never seen anything so marvelous.

"Where is everyone?" Izzy asked.

"It's time for the evening feast," Calla said. "The fairy folk must be gathered at the great dining table. We eat most of our meals together." She flew toward the village.

Brooke and Izzy followed her past the tiny homes and paths until they got to a long wooden table surrounded by fairies. They had hair and skin of all different colors, and charming little outfits.

Their laughter and chatter suddenly stopped.

"It's Calla!" shouted an older fairy.

A young fairy boy pointed at her. "She's back!"

"Who's with her?" asked another.

All the fairies stared at them.

Calla cleared her throat. "Yes, I'm back, and I have two guests with me. This is Brooke, the human who saved my life and earned seven wishes from me, and this is her best friend, Izzy."

Brooke held her breath and crossed her fingers that everything would be okay.

"They're . . . humans?" a fairy shrieked.

"And you gave them wings?" asked another.

"They shouldn't be here!"

"What were you thinking, Calla?"

"Someone get the king!"

A few fairies flew off, while others came closer to them.

Brooke waved. "Hello. We're not here to cause problems." She felt so nervous as the exquisite little creatures examined her.

"We're kind and peaceful," Izzy added.

Fairies squinted at them, tilting their heads for a better look. Soon, they were surrounded by the magical creatures, who poked them and touched their wings.

Izzy laughed. "Stop, you're tickling me!"

Brooke spotted two young fairies with narrowed eyes whispering to each other.

Izzy looked at her. "That's Starla and Jasmine, right?"

Brooke nodded. Those two had been sent searching for Calla right after Brooke saved her. When they found Calla, they had teased her for being discovered by humans. Brooke and Izzy had shooed them away. They certainly didn't look like they were whispering anything nice right now.

Calla bowed her head as fairies kept questioning her. She looked so disappointed.

"Calla is an amazing wish granter!" Brooke said, raising her voice so she could be heard.

"She's very smart, too," Izzy added. "She's working on several books about her time with us humans. And a dragon. We met a dragon, too."

The fairies stopped chattering.

Calla looked up and trembled. An older fairy wearing a big crown flew toward her.

"What is the meaning of this, Calla?" he asked, gesturing to Brooke and Izzy.

"Greetings, King Harlan." Calla clasped her hands in front of her. "I'm sure Starla and Jasmine told you I was saved by a human. I've spent the past two weeks fulfilling her wishes. This was her final one. To visit Fairvana. I had to grant it."

Brooke curtsied while hovering in the air. "We're very excited to be here."

Izzy bowed, then curtsied, then giggled. "I'm sorry. I've never met a king before."

The king's face turned different shades of red before he said, "The three of you need to come with me."

Chapter 4

Brooke gulped as they followed the king away from the banquet table. So much for a great visit. She knew she'd messed this wish up somehow. "I wonder what fairy jail is like?" she whispered to Izzy.

"I hope we don't find out!" Izzy looked terrified.

The king led them into an opening in a huge tree. Inside, the girls could see that the tree was actually a magnificent castle. But

Brooke was too nervous to delight over all the details. The three of them were obviously facing serious trouble.

They followed the king into a room with a big desk and several chairs. "Take a seat," he said, closing the door behind them.

Brooke perched on the edge of a chair as the king took his place behind the desk. At least there weren't any guards in the room, or fairies waiting with handcuffs.

He stared at them, pacing back and forth for a few minutes.

Brooke's throat was tight with fear.

Izzy's eyes were wide, and her wings were thrumming like a hummingbird's.

"It's been hundreds of years since one of

our kind has been discovered by humans," he said.

"Yes, well, it's about time we got some thorough research on the human world, right?" Calla asked nervously. "Things have changed so much since then. They don't use horse-drawn carriages anymore. They have something called cars that zoom along the streets. And giant winged machines that fly in the sky! It's amazing, really."

The king stared at Calla for a long time. Finally, he said, "I'm so envious." A huge smile split his face. "Calla, you must tell me everything! How many humans did you meet? How big are you two normally? Did you try any of their food?" He sank into his

seat and propped his chin up with one hand.
"Tell me all about the human world." He
looked at them dreamily.

Brooke let out the breath she'd been
holding. She and Izzy looked at each other
and tried not to laugh. Brooke cleared
her throat. "So, just to be clear, we're not in
trouble?"

"No, no, no," the king said. "I'm *thrilled* to be meeting humans."

"But what about the rules to never be discovered by us?" Izzy asked.

The king waved his hand in the air. "That's for the safety of all fairies. The forest can be dangerous. And who knows what humans would do to us? We certainly don't want fairies journeying to the human world too often. But Calla appears to be fine, and you like her enough to come to her land."

"So no fairy jail?" Brooke asked.

"No hard labor?" Izzy added.

"Of course not! What do you think I am, a troll? Besides, one of you saved Calla, correct?" he asked.

"Yes—I did," Brooke said. "From my cat."

The king gasped. "A cat?" He turned back to Calla. "Weren't you scared?"

Calla set her hand over her heart. "Terrified. I thought for certain the beast was going to devour me. Death was moments away." She placed the back of her hand over her eyes.

Brooke held back a giggle listening to her exaggerated story.

"You are lucky indeed. Now tell me, what was the food like?"

Calla clapped. "Oh! They have the most delicious treats! Mounds of smooth, brown sweets called chocolate chips. They're huge! And giant blocks of sugar!"

"No!"

Calla nodded. "It was incredible."

"What did you do while you were there?" the king asked her.

"Oh, so many things. I went to school, to the store, and to the bank where they keep their gold. I'm writing several books about everything I've learned."

The king nodded. "Excellent, excellent. And how did the wish granting go?"

"Wonderful!" Calla said.

"Well, she's a great wish granter—they all came true—but I didn't make the best wishes," Brooke added. Although maybe she hadn't screwed up this one after all!

They spent the next hour detailing everything that had happened since Calla arrived in the human world.

The king blinked in astonishment when the three of them were done telling the tale.

"A dragon?" He shook his head. "I cannot believe it. They still exist!" He sighed.

"And now you two girls are living with us. What fun!"

"Oh, we're not living here," Brooke said.

Izzy shook her head. "No, we're just visiting."

"Right, of course." The king stood and leaned against his desk. "Well, this is one of the most exciting things to happen in our land. I'd say this calls for a celebration. A huge feast! A kingdom-wide party—two days from now."

"Two days?" Brooke asked.

"We need time to prepare," the king explained.

"I didn't think we'd be here so long," Izzy said.

"It doesn't matter. Remember, time is paused on your side of the forest," Calla reminded them.

Brooke took Izzy's hand and squeezed it. "Don't worry. It'll be fun!"

Chapter 5

When they flew out of the castle, a huge crowd of fairies was gathered below.

"Are we banishing the humans?" one fairy called out.

"Is Calla in big trouble?" another asked.

The king held out both hands and the crowd quieted. "We are doing none of those things. I have determined this is cause for celebration. We're entering a new age of"—he paused to hold out his arms—"understanding humans."

"That's also the title of my upcoming book!" Calla shouted. "One of many."

"Preparations shall begin for a party two days from now. I want this to be a gala for the history books. School is cancelled for the next week, and all work is to be suspended unless it's for our party. Let the preparations begin!" Then King Harlan clapped his hands twice and returned to his castle.

Calla grabbed Izzy and Brooke by the hand. "Come on! Let me show you my house! And then we have to start planning your party dresses. You can't wear those human clothes."

"Fairy party dresses!" Izzy cried.

She and Brooke shrieked at the same time.

"My parents will be so excited to meet you," Calla said. "I didn't see them at the banquet table. Perhaps they ate at home tonight. Follow me!"

They flew behind Calla as she zipped back to the village of tiny homes. Brooke and Izzy kept hitting each other with their wings by mistake.

"Sorry!" Brooke said.

"Me too," Izzy said. "This is hard." Her wing brushed against Brooke's again and she giggled.

Finally, they got to Calla's cottage, nestled in the roots of a giant tree.

The three of them landed, and Calla took

a deep breath before walking inside. "Mother, Father! I'm home!"

An older fairy with the same blue-colored hair as Calla zoomed to the door. "My darling dear! I've missed you." She hugged Calla and stepped back. "Whatever were you thinking, going to the human world?"

Another fairy, who Brooke guessed was Calla's father, flew into the room. "Young lady, you'd be in big trouble if I weren't so happy to see you." He hugged her. "Are you okay?"

"Yes! I'm great! The human world was wonderful." Calla spun in a circle. "And I made two amazing friends who wanted to come see *our* world. I'd like to introduce Brooke and Izzy."

"It's so nice to meet you," Brooke said, shaking the older fairies' hands.

"You have a lovely home," Izzy said.

"Can they stay with us for a while?" Calla asked. "The king declared that we're having a grand celebration in two days in honor of their visit."

"Of course! Show them to your slumber chamber and I'll get some food for you."

They followed Calla to a room in the back of the house. A canopy bed sat in the middle of the room, made of sticks and bark, covered in moss and tiny flowers. Bits of crystal hung from the canopy. The quilt was made of silky flower petals.

"How beautiful!" Izzy said.

Calla flopped on the bed. "Ahh. I didn't realize how much I missed my milkweed mattress. So cozy! It's big enough that all three of us can sleep here."

"Look!" Brooke said. "Suitcases filled with clothes for us!"

"You did wish for everything we'd need," Izzy said.

A jar filled with glowing sparkles lit up the room. A toadstool chair sat in the corner. The rug was a wonderfully soft, thick piece of moss.

Calla got up and set her notebook on a desk. "I have a lot of writing to do. But that can wait. I'm so excited to show you both everything in Fairvana."

It was dark outside now, and fireflies blinked on and off in the woods. "Maybe we should wait until tomorrow," Brooke said, disappointed. "It's getting late. Are you sure time is paused back home?"

"Of course," Calla said. "There is nothing to worry about."

"Time to eat!" Calla's mother called.

They sat around a tree stump table that was filled with delectable goodies: mushroom soup, a salad of greens and flowers, bowls of nuts.

"Mmm, this is so good!" Izzy said.

"Thank you for letting us stay here," Brooke said between mouthfuls.

"You can stay as long as you'd like," Calla's mom said.

"We have lots of exploring to do tomorrow," Calla told them. "And so much work to do for the party!"

After dinner, they tumbled into Calla's bed, giggling and bopping each other with the soft down pillows. Brooke's wings got hit and bent a few times, but they easily straightened back into place. It was still so strange to have wings!

It wasn't long before they snuggled under the covers. Calla immediately started snoring. Brooke and Izzy giggled softly, and soon Izzy's breathing evened out.

But Brooke lay awake, and not just because it was hard to get comfortable lying on her wings. Even though time back home was paused, Brooke couldn't stop wondering if everything was okay. She wasn't sure how Calla had paused time. What if she'd done it wrong and Brooke's mom was worried about her?

And she still had a bad feeling she'd forgotten a very important part of the wish. Like Izzy, she hadn't thought they'd be gone two whole days. Brooke had never been away from her mother for that long.

She blew out a deep breath and reminded herself to enjoy her time here. They were the only humans who'd ever visited Fairvana! And tomorrow, it was time to start planning a party for the fairy history books.

Chapter 6

The sun had just risen and Calla was shaking Brooke and Izzy awake. "Time to get up! I want to show you everything!"

Izzy sat straight up in bed. "We're really here? In Fairvana? I thought it was a dream!"

"Nope, just the best wish ever by yours truly." Brooke gave her friend a high five.

They grabbed some nuts and berries on their way out the door and flew toward the village. Calla pointed out the flower shop, the toadstoolery, the food market, and the dressmaker. "We'll stop there later. First, I want to show you something neat!"

Brooke laughed. "This is *all* neat!"

They flew into the forest, and Calla stopped next to an old wishing well. It was nestled behind a rotting tree. A big mirror hung from the tree, but it was broken. It didn't look like anyone had been back here in a long time.

"What is this?" Izzy asked.

"It's one of the places where wishes from the human world end up." Calla lowered the bucket into the well. When she pulled it back up, it was full of coins.

"Those are all people's wishes?" Brooke asked. "Are you going to grant them?"

Calla shook her head. "Wishes show up here as coins in the well, but we stopped granting them long before I was born."

"Why?"

Calla shrugged. "Lots of reasons. For one, most of the wishes can't be granted." Calla picked up a coin and tapped it three times with her finger. "Reveal your wish!"

A little boy's voice started talking. "I wish my dog didn't die."

Calla frowned. "It's really sad not being able to grant that wish. But, as I told you before, there are rules. So, some of the wishes made the fairies sad. Others made them mad because of their selfishness." She grabbed another coin and tapped it. "Reveal your wish."

A grown-up man's voice said, "I wish Sally loved me instead of Roger."

Calla shrugged. "We can't grant a wish like that, either. As the years went on, fairies got discouraged, so the tradition of wish granting was abandoned." She bowed her head. "I think that's why so many fairies are upset with me, because I granted wishes to a human."

"I'm sorry." Brooke felt horrible.

"Don't be. It's the law." Calla's smile returned. "Besides, it was fun!"

"Why is there a mirror back here?" Izzy asked.

"My mother told me that when the fairies were granting wishes, they could see the wish come true in that mirror," Calla explained. "But a branch hit it during a great storm, and no one could fix it."

"Could you grant one of these wishes right now if you wanted to?" Izzy asked.

Calla shrugged. "Sure." She grabbed another coin, tapped it three times, and said, "Reveal your wish."

They heard a young woman's voice say, "I wish I could find my missing pearl ring."

Calla rubbed her hands together and a flash of glitter filled the air. "You can't see it in the mirror anymore, but her wish has been granted."

Izzy and Brooke blinked at each other. "Cool!" they both said.

"Come on, there's more to see!" Calla shouted, flying away from the wishing well.

They followed Calla and stopped at a beautiful waterfall. She crouched behind the shrubs surrounding the pool of water. "Water sprites like to dance here first thing in the morning."

Brooke held her breath as five tiny, iridescent creatures rode leaf boats over the falls.

The boats bobbed onto the water as they tumbled over the falls. The sprites stepped out of their boats and skated across the surface, twirling and dancing gracefully.

Brooke held her breath as she watched the incredible show. She was so glad she'd made the wish to come here. It was amazing.

A rustling noise was coming from the woods, and the sprites stopped dancing.

They fled from the water into the woods on the other side of the river.

Brooke, Izzy, and Calla turned to see what was making such a racket. Calla moaned. "Ugh. The very last fairies I want to see."

Brooke saw two fairies flying their way, chattering and laughing loudly. "It's Starla and Jasmine."

"There you are," Starla called, spotting Calla. "I can't believe you brought these humans home with you."

"The king was very excited to meet my friends," Calla retorted. "I'm sure you heard about the party."

The two nasty fairies laughed. "Can't believe you had to go all the way to the human world to find friends," Jasmine sneered.

Brooke grabbed Calla by the arm. "Come on, let's go back to the village. Don't listen to them."

They flew off toward the village and saw the great banquet table filled with fairies again.

"Can we eat breakfast?" Izzy asked. "I'm starving."

They flew toward the table and everyone stopped talking. Then a few of the fairies smiled. A few more even flew up out of their seats. "Calla! Come sit by us," said one fairy, patting the seat next to her.

"No, sit by us!"

Calla's cheeks turned red. "I'm not used to anyone wanting to sit by me."

Brooke and Izzy shared a smile. "Not everyone is mean like Starla and Jasmine," Brooke whispered back. "I think things are going to be a lot different for you now, Calla."

Chapter 7

A small fairy with curly orange hair flew over and grabbed Calla by the hand. Flowers were tucked in among her curls, and she had a big, determined smile on her face. "You and your friends are sitting with *me*," she said.

They followed her to the log bench next to the table and sat down.

The fairy shook hands with Brooke and Izzy. "I'm Magnolia! Nice to meet you."

"You too," Brooke said.

"You've got the coolest hair!" Izzy said.

Magnolia patted it. "I know! Thanks!"

Calla leaned over and whispered to Brooke, "She's the most popular fairy in the whole village!"

Magnolia pulled a flower from her hair and started plucking the petals. "I didn't believe Starla and Jasmine when they said you got discovered by humans. I thought you just ran away or were sulking somewhere in the woods. But you did it! You really did it! You granted seven wishes and lived in the human world for two weeks?"

The fairies at the table gathered closer.

Calla told the whole story again while they ate breakfast. Every fairy was listening with wide eyes.

When she got to the part about the dragon, Magnolia's jaw dropped. She looked at Brooke. "You walked up to a dragon?"

Brooke nodded. "I had to. Otherwise she was going to scorch my meadow."

"They are extraordinary humans," Calla said.

Brooke's cheeks felt hot. Izzy grinned her biggest grin.

"Then we must make sure you two have the most beautiful gowns ever for the party," Magnolia said. "Come on, Calla. Let's get to the dressmaker's shop!" Magnolia zoomed into the air, and Calla followed her.

Brooke and Izzy trailed behind. "We're still slow, but we're getting better at this," Izzy said as they flew into the village.

"It's going to be so weird when we go back home and can only walk!" Brooke said.

"No going home yet!" Calla said happily. "You can't leave before the party!"

They landed in front of an exquisite little store with beautiful dresses displayed in the windows. Then they walked inside and gasped. Vines and garlands of flowers hung from the ceiling. Butterflies swarmed overhead. Gorgeous materials were stacked up on tables: shaggy fabric made from yellow dandelions, rose petals woven into a delicate pale pink cloth, flattened cocoons dyed bright blue, and so many others.

Brooke sucked in a breath. "I've never seen such interesting materials!"

"Well, I still love the dresses from your

dollhouse," Calla said. "There's nothing like that here."

A fairy wearing a white dress with golden leaves sewn onto it flew over to them. "Hello, darlings! My name is Tatiana, and I own this shop. Please, pick out whatever you'd like. My treat! I'll be the first fairy in history to make gowns for humans! They will be my best designs yet!"

Brooke and Izzy squealed.

"And you're getting a dress, too," Tatiana said to Calla. "We wouldn't be having this grand celebration if it weren't for you! I had to hire five extra fairies to keep up with all my new dress orders."

Calla twirled. "Amazing! Thank you!"

Brooke, Izzy, Magnolia, and Calla examined every piece of fabric in the store, every bauble and bead.

"It's so hard to decide!" Brooke said.

They tried on fancy accessories and dresses, modeling for the fairies who crowded the store to watch.

After an hour or so, Izzy picked out the yellow dandelion fabric. Brooke chose a beautiful white silk made of milkweed, and Calla selected a wildflower material.

"These are going to be beautiful!" Izzy said.

Tatiana promised to have them finished by the next morning.

"I can't wait for the party tomorrow night!" Calla said.

Brooke bit her lip. "Will we be going home after that?"

"It'll be well past midnight when the

party ends," Calla said. "We don't want to fly through the woods in the dark."

"So the next morning?" Brooke missed her mom. She missed Patches. She wasn't used to all this attention, either. It wasn't as bad as when she'd wished to be popular, but she was starting to feel overwhelmed.

"We'll just have to see!" Calla said. "But why do you want to leave? There's so much more to explore and do. Everything is fine back home. Time is frozen. You can stay here as long as you want."

Brooke tried to ignore the bad feeling in her stomach. All of her other wishes had gone so wrong. It seemed pretty likely something with this one would get messed up, too.

But how?

Chapter 8

After a delicious dinner of acorn soup and herb pie, the fairies gathered around a bonfire, asking Brooke and Izzy questions about the human world. Even the moths fluttering about and the owls hooting in the trees seemed to pause and listen.

Calla sat between the two of them, beaming.

"If you don't fly, how do you get around

quickly?" Magnolia asked. "Walking is so slow."

"We both have bicycles," Brooke said, explaining how bicycles worked.

"And cars," Izzy said. "Cars can go very fast. Fifty miles an hour!"

The fairies gasped.

Brooke and Izzy answered questions about their school and the library. They taught the fairies how to high-five.

Magnolia sighed. "I want to go to the human world." Several other fairies nodded in agreement.

"Tomorrow, the four of us must get ready for the party together so you can tell me more."

"Oh, but I was going to ask them to come to my house for tea!" said a fairy named Daisy.

"And I've been baking sweets just for them," said another fairy.

Calla's smile had never been bigger. "We'll be sure to stop by and visit anyone who wants us to."

It was a busy day visiting with all the fairies who had brewed special tea and made delicacies like violet candies and rose muffins. They were so busy, Brooke didn't even have time to worry. Before she knew it, the sun was setting. The party would begin soon!

"We have to get ready! Let's pick up our dresses," Calla said.

"My new dress is there, too," Magnolia said. "We'll get ready at the store!"

They hurried to the shop, where their beautiful dresses waited.

Brooke sucked in a deep breath as she looked at hers. "I've never seen anything so beautiful." The silky milkweed material had been transformed into a sweeping gown. White feathers trimmed the bottom, and white rose petals graced the top. She rushed into a dressing room to change. When she came out, she twirled and twirled, laughing the whole time.

Izzy clapped. "It's gorgeous! Imagine if you'd had this for the chorus concert!"

"Try on yours!" Brooke said.

Izzy came out of the dressing room

beaming. The fringy yellow skirt swished happily around her legs. Green leaves made the top look like a flower ready to bloom.

"Spectacular!" Magnolia shouted. "Come on, Calla, let's get changed."

Magnolia came out in a shiny bright purple dress. "No one's going to miss me in this!"

"It's beautiful!" Brooke said.

Then Calla came out in the most beautiful dress of all. Layers of the wildflower
material had been sewn into a long gown
that swept the floor as she walked.

"You look like a princess!" Izzy
whispered.

"And now for the accessories!" Tatiana

announced, setting boxes and baskets of trinkets and jewels on a table.

Brooke twined a flowery vine up one arm. Izzy chose a lovely necklace with an amber pendant. Calla placed a crown of flowers on her head, and Magnolia stuck crystals and flowers in every curl of her hair.

"You'll be the belles of the ball!" Tatiana declared. "Now go have fun! I'll see you at the party."

They flew to the great banquet table, where a grand feast would kick off the celebration. Huge bonfires at both ends of the table lit up the night.

Branches of pussy willow arched over the table. Flowers and bits of crystal were woven into the branches. Lanterns hung from the arches, casting a beautiful golden glow. The girls sat down and marveled at every little detail, and soon, fairies were crowding around them, chatting excitedly.

"This is way better than Emily's birthday party," Izzy whispered to Brooke.

Wide-eyed, Brooke nodded. "Definitely." She sipped the delicious rosewater punch as the table filled up with beautifully dressed fairies.

The king flew to the head of the table, and the crowd quieted. "Welcome to this most amazing night. For the first time in our history, we have human visitors. A special reason indeed to celebrate." He turned to

Calla. "Could you and your friends join me, please?"

Calla nodded, and the three of them flew to join the king.

"I hereby make Brooke and Izzy official residents of Fairvana. And Calla, you will have a special place in our history books for forging this new relationship with the humans."

The three of them held hands and grinned, while the crowd cheered.

"Brooke and Izzy, I look forward to many interesting conversations with you," the king said.

"Thank you so much," Brooke said. "We have loved our visit, and we are going to enjoy our last night here most of all, I think."

The king looked confused, and the fairies below them whispered as Brooke, Izzy, and Calla flew back to their seats.

"Let the festivities begin!" the king declared.

Tiny mice brought out trays of bread and soups. A troupe of fairies with delicate flutes and chimes hovered in the air playing sweet music. Then a pack of wisps appeared, dancing and bobbing to the tune.

"They're so cute!" Izzy said.

When the wisps' performance ended and the soup bowls were empty, platters of cheese and nuts appeared. Brooke and Izzy filled their plates and enjoyed the treats while fairies holding fiery torches danced overhead.

When dinner was finished, baker fairies brought out a towering cake covered in berries and flowers.

The food and the performances went on for hours. Then it was time for dancing.

Brooke and Izzy weren't as graceful as most of the fairies pirouetting in the air, so they grabbed on to each other's hands and spun in circles, howling in delight. Soon all the fairies were doing it, too.

Magnolia showed them how to use their wings to zoom straight up in the air. It was exhilarating.

By the time the party was over, they'd met every fairy who lived in the village. They even had a special dance with the king. And Calla was the center of attention, smiling the entire night.

By the time they flew back to Calla's house, the girls were so exhausted they collapsed into bed without even changing out of their beautiful gowns.

"That was wonderful," Brooke said.

Izzy nodded. "The best night of my life."

"I think we're ready to go back tomorrow," Brooke said, snuggling up in bed.

Called yawned and said, "Maybe," then quickly started snoring.

Brooke gave Izzy a worried look. "What does she mean, *maybe*?"

Chapter 9

They slept in until lunchtime the next day. Brooke bolted out of bed, alarmed at how high in the sky the sun was. "We should get going if we want to get home before dark," she said.

Calla yawned and stretched lazily. "I'm too tired to fly back today. Besides, I haven't shown you how we harvest the nectar from the dancing morning glories. It's tricky, because they're quick!"

Brooke was worried about the trip home, but she really did want to see dancing flowers.

Izzy squealed. "That will be so fun!"

They changed out of their gowns and headed out of the village. Two fairies were ahead of them, flying toward the archway that led out of the kingdom.

"That's Starla and Jasmine!" Calla said, flying after them.

Brooke and Izzy chased after Calla.

"Where are you guys going?" Calla asked the two fairies.

Starla rolled her eyes. "We're sick of you getting all this attention just for granting a few wishes."

"We can do that, too," Jasmine said.

Starla rolled her eyes. "And we'll be even better at it."

"But it can be very dangerous," Calla said.

"You just want all the glory for yourself," Jasmine said.

"See you later!" Starla said as they slipped through the tiny opening.

"I've got to tell the king!" Calla cried.

They flew to the palace and asked to see him immediately.

He quickly came out, yawning and smiling. "What a party that was."

"It was lovely," Calla said. "But sir, I thought you should know Starla and Jasmine just left Fairvana, headed for the human world. They want to grant wishes, too!"

"But that's very dangerous!"

"They're jealous of all the attention Calla's been getting," Izzy explained.

"I must send someone after them right away," the king said. "Thank you for letting me know."

"You're welcome!" Brooke said. "Let's go see those dancing flowers, and then we can get going, too."

But a group of fairies stopped them before they could get very far. "Calla, tell us more about the books you're writing!"

"Oh, of course!" Calla said happily. She sat down on one of the benches in the middle of the village and chatted on and on. When the first group left, another showed up, sharing treats and sweets.

"Calla, I'm so glad we've become good friends," Magnolia said. "I always thought you were so interested in the human world, you didn't care if you had fairy friends."

Calla beamed. "I'm so happy to have forged a friendship, too."

The afternoon slipped away as fairies stopped to talk to them and Calla answered every question.

Brooke didn't want to interrupt Calla's fun and demand she take them home. It was nice to see her finally making some good friends in the fairy world. But then another day slipped by too quickly.

"Wow, the day flew by," Calla finally said. "We'll go see the dancing morning glories tomorrow."

Brooke frowned. "I'd rather just go home first thing tomorrow."

"Oh! Don't you like it here?" Calla asked.

"I do, but I've never been away from home this long before."

Just then, Starla and Jasmine flew back into the village, their heads hanging. They spotted Calla, and Starla pointed at her. "You told on us!"

"I was worried you two would get hurt," Calla said.

"We just wanted to learn more about the human world firsthand," Jasmine said. The two of them zoomed off in a huff.

"See?" Brooke said. "We should go. Our visit here is starting to cause problems."

Calla sighed. "Very well. I'll take you home tomorrow."

But the next day, they woke up to thunder booming through the little village and lightning flashing in the sky. Rain poured so hard, they couldn't even go outside. "We can't make the trip today. It's too hard to fly when your wings are wet," Calla said. "I'm going to work on my books."

Brooke and Izzy sat on Calla's bed watching the rain stream down the windows while she wrote.

"I miss riding bikes," Izzy said.

Brooke nodded and sighed. "I miss sleeping in my own bed."

But the next day when they asked Calla to leave, they were stopped by a parade marching through the village in their honor. It would be rude to leave then.

And the next day as they tried to return home, all the fairies were gathered on the edge of town.

Magnolia waved them over. "Come here, you won't believe it!"

They flew over to the scene—a baby unicorn was galloping in a circle, doing tricks.

"A baby unicorn?" Calla looked so stunned she almost dropped to the ground. "Never in the kingdom's history have we seen a baby unicorn. We can't leave now!"

And while it was fun to watch the cute little guy's antics, Brooke was getting that bad feeling in her stomach again.

"I feel like there's a reason we can't go home. Like something's keeping us from going," she whispered to Izzy that night as they tried to sleep. Brooke sat up, her wings quivering.

"Take a few deep breaths. That always helps me," Izzy said.

Brooke nodded and followed Izzy's advice. She did feel a bit better. But she still wanted to go home.

"We need to talk to Calla first thing tomorrow," Brooke said.

"Let's go look for dryads," Calla said after breakfast. "They're much friendlier in Fairvana than the ones we found by your stream."

"No," Brooke said. "It sounds fun, but I really want to go home. Now."

"We just wanted to come for a short visit," Izzy explained.

Calla frowned. "Let's get you home, then."

Brooke and Izzy shared a high five and followed Calla to the tiny opening that led out of the kingdom. They were almost there when Calla stopped flying. "I don't believe it."

Brooke groaned. "What?"

Calla pointed to the archway. "Someone's boarded it up! That's the only way out."

Chapter 10

Brooke looked at the wood nailed over the opening between the trees. "Who would do that?"

"I don't know," Calla said. "We should go tell King Harlan."

They flew to the castle, and Brooke was feeling more and more nervous. Why were they having such a hard time leaving Fairvana?

She stopped flying, and her mouth

dropped open. "Oh no," she whispered to herself.

Calla and Izzy stopped flying, too, and came over to her. "What's wrong?" Izzy asked.

"I forgot something very important in my wish," Brooke said.

Calla cocked her head. "What could it possibly be? You were quite thorough."

Brooke closed her eyes and sighed. "I said that we wanted to *visit* Fairvana. But I never said for how *long*. Maybe we're stuck here!"

Calla tapped her finger against her nose, thinking. "Hmm. That might indeed explain the troubles you've been having. Perhaps the wish doesn't want you to leave! Let's ask the king about this, too."

They flew to the castle and were immediately brought to the king's chambers.

He stood up from his throne and smiled. "What brings you here today?"

Calla stepped forward. "My friends are trying to return to the human world, but we keep getting stalled." She looked down. "I admit, I organized the parade hoping to keep you here longer. But I didn't do any of the other things. Magnolia's the one who found the baby unicorn and brought it to the village."

The king nodded. "And I caused the storm."

"Really?" Izzy asked. "You can do that?"

"His magic is very powerful," Calla said.

"But this morning, I found the archway boarded up! Now they can't leave."

"Who would do such a thing?" Brooke asked.

The king paused. "Why, I did that, too."

"What?" Calla gasped.

"You mean to imprison us here?" Brooke asked.

"No!" The king laughed. "You're welcome

to stay here as long as you like. You're official citizens of Fairvana, after all."

"Then why did you board up the exit?" Izzy asked.

"To keep the other fairies from leaving," he said. "So many fairies have been caught trying to sneak off to the human world. But it's too dangerous! For their own good, the exit has been blocked."

"Can you unblock it for us?" Brooke asked.

"I'll unblock it soon, but for now, I think the best plan is for you to visit with the fairies so they get their fill of the human world. Then they'll get bored with the whole idea of meeting humans and granting wishes."

Brooke felt her eyes tearing up. "I really miss my home."

"You'll be back soon enough. Enjoy your time here. We can schedule another feast in a fortnight if you'd like," the king said.

"Two more weeks!" Izzy exclaimed. "But I'm homesick, too."

The king gestured to the door. "I'll let you know when I reopen the archway. In the meantime, I'll address the fairy kingdom, letting everyone know that no one is to leave Fairvana until I say so."

The three of them left and hovered outside the castle. "I'm sorry," Calla said.

"It's not your fault," Brooke said.

"Hey, I've got an idea," Izzy said. "Maybe you could quickly finish writing your books, and then fairies could read them instead of visiting our world."

"That's genius!" Brooke said.

"Do you know how long it takes to write a book?" Calla asked. "Long! I had no idea. Who knew it could be so complicated!"

"There's got to be a solution!" Brooke said. "I wish I had another wish."

"Sorry, I can't grant another," Calla said. "Though I think that's what the fairies are really after. The thrill of wish granting."

Izzy looked confused. "Then why don't they just go to that old wishing well and grant a few?"

"I told you, we don't do that anymore," Calla said.

A huge smile grew on Brooke's face. "But what if you tried it again?"

Chapter 11

They invited Magnolia and a few other fairies to join them for an adventure.

"Where are we going?" Magnolia asked. "The king sealed off the exit, so we're stuck here in Fairvana."

"Just follow us!" Calla said.

The group flew to the old wishing well, and Magnolia frowned. "What are we doing here? No one uses the wishing well anymore."

"But maybe we should," Calla said. "It's really no different than what I did with Brooke, is it? Try one!"

Brooke crossed her fingers. If Magnolia thought granting these wishes was fun, everyone would want to do it.

Magnolia picked up a coin from the ground and tapped it three times. "Reveal your wish."

A young man's voice said, "I wish I was taller."

Magnolia frowned. "I can't grant that. See, this isn't fun."

"Try again!" Brooke said.

She selected another coin, and this one played the voice of a little girl saying, "I wish I had a puppy."

Magnolia's eyes widened. "I can do that one!" She rubbed her hands together and glitter exploded in the air. "Your wish has been granted." Magnolia smiled, looking around. "Did it work?"

One of the other fairies frowned. "How will we ever know? The mirror is broken."

Brooke and Izzy looked at each other. "What if you fixed the mirror?"

"That's a great question for the king," Calla said.

After they flew to the castle and told the king their idea, he immediately returned with them to the wishing well.

"I'm not sure if this will work, but it's worth a try." He cleared his throat and rubbed his hands together. "Repair this mirror with a view to the human world and the wishes being granted!"

A cloud of glitter blinded them for a moment, but when it cleared, the mirror was still broken.

The king frowned. "I was hoping the presence of two humans would provide the link to the human world we need to fix this."

"What if we touched the mirror while you tried to cast the spell?" Brooke asked.

"We could try that," the king said.

Brooke and Izzy walked to the mirror, and they each grabbed one side of it. The king repeated his spell. But that didn't work, either.

"It's no use," the king said.

"Wait," Brooke said. "Maybe we need someone from the fairy world to complete the link. Calla, grab our hands."

Calla hurried over and grabbed the girls' hands.

The king did the spell once more, and this time, when the glitter cleared, the mirror was no longer cracked.

"I think it worked!" Calla said. "Let's try

it out." She grabbed a coin from the ground and tapped it three times. "Reveal your wish!"

A little boy's voice said, "I wish I had a new bike."

The mirror went foggy for a moment, but then it cleared and showed a little boy finding a shiny red bike in his front yard.

"It worked!" the king said.

Fairies started grabbing coins from the ground and revealing the wishes.

"Reveal your wish!" said Daisy.

"I wish my hair was three feet long," said a woman's voice.

After an explosion of glitter, the lady appeared in the mirror, and her short hair grew past her shoulders, down to the middle of her back.

"Look how happy she is!" Daisy said. "That was fun!"

The king turned to Brooke, Izzy, and Calla. "You did it. The fairies are enjoying wish granting again—and humans are finally getting their wishes fulfilled. You came up with a solution to make everyone happy."

"I told you guys they were exceptional humans," Calla said.

Brooke and Izzy each put an arm around Calla. "Thanks," they both said.

"Can we go home now?" Brooke said. "Can you open the exit, King Harlan?"

Chapter 12

The king unsealed the exit, and fairies crowded around the door, waving goodbye.

"We'll never forget our visit here," Brooke said.

"We'll miss you!" Izzy said as they flew through the door into the magical forest.

On the way back, they made sure to fly out of their way to avoid the trolls. Soon,

Brooke started recognizing the trees and clearings that were close to her home. "We're almost there!"

They flew out of the forest and landed before they crossed the stream. The butterfly was still suspended in the air. Patches was still frozen, mid-lick, on the rock.

"Once we get to the other side, time starts again," Calla said. "Your wings disappear, and you'll get big. Are you ready?"

Brooke was going to miss her wings, but she nodded. "Yes!"

"Let's go home!" Izzy said.

"Wait!" Calla cried. "One last thing."

Brooke blew out a frustrated breath. They were so close! "What now?"

Calla softened her voice. "I was hoping to get one last hug while we're all still little."

Brooke felt horrible for sounding snippy. She walked over and hugged Calla. "Thanks for everything." She stepped back and smiled.

Izzy threw her arms around Calla. "I'm going to miss you so much."

Calla wiped away tears as they stood there. "I'm so glad your cat almost killed me." The three of them laughed. Then they flew across the stream.

The butterfly started flying again. Patches sat up and stretched. Pumpkin's ears twitched.

Brooke and Izzy started growing bigger

and bigger. They squealed as their arms swelled back to their normal size. They gasped as their legs touched the ground. And then, with a poof of fairy dust, their wings disappeared.

Izzy spun around, trying to check her back. "They're gone!"

Brooke scooped up Patches and kissed her head. "I missed you so much."

Izzy picked up Pumpkin and held her tight.

"Come on!" Brooke started running toward her house.

Izzy followed, then turned around. "Where's Calla?"

The fairy hovered by the stream.

They went back to her. "Aren't you coming?" Brooke asked.

Calla frowned. "I've completed all my wishes. It's time for me to go home now."

"Can't you stay?" Izzy asked.

Brooke blinked back tears. "Won't we ever see you again?"

Calla shook her head. "It's too risky. I might be discovered again, by someone not as nice as you two. And I have new friends back home to visit. But I will miss you."

Brooke thought for a moment, then snapped her fingers. "What if we met you on the other side of the stream? The magical side?"

"Maybe, but how will you know when I'm visiting?" Calla asked.

"Too bad there isn't some way to let us know when you're there," Izzy said.

Calla flew up into the air and twirled around. "The wisps! They could blink on and off by the edge of the stream when I come to visit. Then you can come over to the magical side and see me."

"Great idea!" Brooke beamed. "We'll watch for the wisps."

"Come back and visit soon," Izzy said.

"I will. I promise. After all, you are official residents of Fairvana. Technically, you'll be fairies forever. I should check up on you." Calla winked at them.

Brooke and Izzy smiled as Calla zoomed back toward the magical forest and disappeared in the trees.

Brooke and Izzy looked at each other. "It certainly was exciting," Izzy said. "All of it, from the very first wish."

"I'm so glad we got to experience it together," Brooke said.

"Come on!" Izzy said, running toward Brooke's house.

They dashed in through the back door.

"Mom?" Brooke called. "Where are you?"

"In the living room." Her mom's voice sounded strange.

Brooke and Izzy shared a concerned look and hurried to the living room, where Brooke's mom sat on the couch.

Brooke scooted onto the couch next to her and gave her mom a huge hug. "I missed you so much!"

"You only went outside fifteen minutes ago," her mom said, confused.

"Right," Brooke said. "It just seems like a long time."

Her mom was studying something she held in her hand.

"What's that?" Brooke asked.

Her mom shook her head. "It's the craziest thing. Craziest." She opened her hand. It was a pretty silver ring with a pearl mounted in a ring of diamonds. "I lost this ring in high school. And I just found it on the floor."

Brooke and Izzy looked at each other, their eyes bulging.

"You grew up in this house, right?" Izzy asked.

Brooke's mom nodded. "But I looked everywhere for this ring. I got it from my parents for my graduation and lost it a month later. That was years ago. I looked and wished to find it, but no luck. How did it just turn up now?"

Brooke shrugged. "I guess some wishes take a while to come true."

Her mom slid the ring on her finger and held out her hand. "I'm so happy it finally did." She smiled. "I should make more wishes."

Brooke and Izzy looked at each other and tried not to laugh.

"Nah," Brooke said. "Our life is pretty great already."

Her mom looped an arm around her for a hug. "You're right."

Brooke leaned against her mother and grabbed Izzy's hand. Patches rubbed up against her legs. There was no wish in the world that could make her happier than she was right then.

The Wish Fairy

One tiny fairy. Seven big wishes!

The Wish Fairy — Too Many Cats! — Lisa Ann Scott

The Wish Fairy — The Treasure Trap — Lisa Ann Scott

The Wish Fairy — Perfectly Popular — Lisa Ann Scott

The Wish Fairy — Fairies Forever — Lisa Ann Scott

WISHFAIRY

Welcome to the
ENCHANTED PONY ACADEMY,
where dreams sparkle and magic shines!